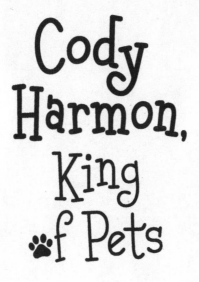

Cody Harmon, King of Pets

Franklin School Friends

Cody Harmon, King of Pets

Claudia Mills

pictures by Rob Shepperson

SQUARE
FISH

Margaret Ferguson Books
Farrar Straus Giroux • New York

SQUARE
FISH

An imprint of Macmillan Publishing Group, LLC
175 Fifth Avenue
New York, NY 10010
mackids.com

Our books may be purchased in bulk for promotional, educational, or
business use. Please contact your local bookseller or the Macmillan Corporate
and Premium Sales Department at (800) 221-7945 ext. 5442 or by e-mail at
MacmillanSpecialMarkets@macmillan.com.

Library of Congress Cataloging-in-Publication Data

Names: Mills, Claudia. | Shepperson, Rob, illustrator.
Title: Cody Harmon, king of pets / Claudia Mills ; pictures by
Rob Shepperson.
Description: New York : Farrar Straus Giroux, 2016. |
Series: Franklin School friends ; 5 | "Margaret Ferguson Books." |
Summary: "Cody Harmon loves animals—he even has nine
pets—so when the school holds a pet show fundraiser, it should
be his time to shine"—Provided by publisher.
Identifiers: LCCN 2015017955 | ISBN 978-1-250-12880-5 (paperback)
ISBN 978-0-374-30224-5 (ebook)
Subjects: CYAC: Pets—Fiction. | Schools—Fiction. | Friendship—
Fiction. | Pet shows—Fiction. | BISAC: JUVENILE FICTION /
School & Education. | JUVENILE FICTION / Social Issues /
Friendship.
Classification: LCC PZ7.M63963 Cod 2016 | DDC [Fic]—dc23
LC record available at http://lccn.loc.gov/2015017955

Originally published in the United States by Farrar Straus Giroux
First Square Fish Edition: 2017
Square Fish logo designed by Filomena Tuosto

3 5 7 9 10 8 6 4

In memory of Michelle Begley,
who knew more about roosters than I ever will,
and to her daughter, Ellen Pumphrey,
with love
—C.M.

For Mark
—R.S.

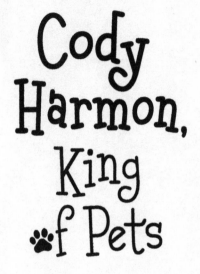

Cody Harmon, King of Pets

1

As Cody Harmon lay on the family room couch after dinner on Sunday evening, his calico cat, Puffball, purred on his chest. His tabby cat, Furface, kneaded his stomach. Rex the golden retriever snored at his feet. And Angus the terrier had just upended the wastepaper basket and was shredding wadded-up tissues all over the family room carpet.

"Angus, no!" Cody hollered.

The cats leaped at the sound. The sheaf of papers on which Cody had been making pig doodles, when he was supposed to be writing a three-page animal report for his teacher, Mrs. Molina, scattered onto the floor.

"Oh, Angus, look what you did!"

Shoving the dog out of the way, Cody started scooping up tissue bits, crumpled wrappers, and the small stuffed giraffe Angus had already destroyed that afternoon. But Cody wasn't mad. He would rather clean up dog mess—even dog poop—than write an animal report any day.

Cody loved animals, all animals.

He did not love writing reports about animals. Especially a report assigned three weeks ago that he had barely begun. Especially a report that was due tomorrow.

His mother came into the room, a baby on each hip: Cody's twin sisters, nine months old and starting to crawl all over the house. Tibbie and Libbie were almost like two more pets, in addition to the dogs, cats, bantam rooster, chickens, and enormous pig out in the pigsty.

"What did he do now?" Cody's mom demanded.

"Nothing," Cody said quickly. "Just got into the trash, but I cleaned it up already."

"That dog is nothing but trouble!" Her eyes fell on the papers still littering the floor, which Angus was now sniffing. "I thought you didn't have any homework this weekend."

"It's not really *homework*. It's an animal report."

"Well, good for you for starting it nice and early." She paused. "When is it due?"

Cody knew better than to lie. "Well, Monday, but—"

"Tomorrow?"

What could Cody say but "I forgot"?

And he *had* forgotten. He'd been busy the whole weekend. A soccer game with his best friend, Tobit Johnson. Helping his mother with the babies. Helping his dad plant the corn. Riding in his dad's pickup to town to spend his twenty dollars of birthday money on tease toys for the cats, squeaker balls for the dogs, and hoof conditioner for Mr. Piggins. How was he supposed to write a pig report, too?

His dad poked his head into the family room doorway. "Everything okay?" he asked with a slow smile.

"Cody has a report due tomorrow," his mom said. "And he hasn't even started it. Have you?" She turned to Cody. "Don't bother answering. I know you haven't."

Well, he had *started* it. Mrs. Molina had made them pick their animal, so he had picked pigs. And she had made them get library books and write a list of the kind of facts they were supposed to find: size, diet, life span, habitat. His books and list were still in his desk at school, buried under all the other work he hadn't remembered to bring home.

"Well, it's only six-thirty now," his dad said mildly. "Bedtime's not for another hour and a half. Let's clear out this menagerie and give the boy a chance to get this thing done."

"Can the animals stay?" Cody asked. "It's a report *on* animals."

His mom harrumphed, but his dad said, "Sure. Just do your best," and gave him another smile.

His dad's encouragement almost made Cody wish he had been working on his report harder.

Back on the couch, with the cats in place and Angus whining to have the squeaker ball tossed for him, Cody looked at Mrs. Molina's assignment sheet. Awake now, Rex nuzzled Cody's knee, as if worried that his boy had such a big report to write so quickly.

"You must get your animal facts from at least two different sources. These must be books or magazines, not the Internet," read the instructions.

Cody doubted everyone in his class would do that. Perfect Simon Ellis would have ten—or twenty, or a hundred—sources, but no one else in the Franklin School third grade was like Simon. Well, Kelsey Green would have a lot of sources, too. Kelsey loved to read. But Tobit probably only had one.

Zero wasn't that much less than one.

Besides, if there was one thing Cody knew about, it was pigs. He could be his own source.

He picked up his pencil and started writing.

I like pigs. Pigs are smart. People think pigs are dirty, but pigs are clean. I like pigs a LOT.

That was a good start.

Pigs eat slops from a trough. My pig is called Mr. Piggins.

Six whole sentences! That was long enough for one page, and he could add another page with a picture. Cody set his completed page on the floor and, on a second sheet of paper, started to draw a portrait of Mr. Piggins from memory.

It wasn't like he'd get a good grade anyway. Mrs. Molina never gave him good grades on anything. He had the worst grades in the class, even worse than Tobit's.

But no one else had as many pets as he did.

Cody looked over at Angus, who had pieces of something white and crumpled hanging out of his mouth. Pieces of Cody's pig report.

"Angus, no!"

It was too late.

Now he had to write the whole dumb report all over again.

At school on Monday, Mrs. Molina collected the animal reports first thing.

"How long was yours?" Cody whispered to Tobit.

Tobit shrugged as if to say, *Who cares?* Then he said, "Two and a half pages. But I wrote really big."

Mrs. Molina had just finished setting the pile of reports on her desk when Mr. Boone, the Franklin School principal, came into the room. Cody relaxed. Some schools had principals who yelled at kids like him and Tobit, whose reports were too short, but Mr. Boone was funny and jolly.

Today, instead of wearing his principal jacket and tie, Mr. Boone wore a T-shirt that said SUPPORT YOUR HUMANE SOCIETY! Cody had adopted his dogs and cats from the Humane Society, though his mother kept threatening to make him take Angus back. Maybe he could support the Humane Society even more by adopting extra pets. A rabbit, maybe. Or a goat!

"Boys and girls!" Mr. Boone boomed. "Next week is going to be a very special week at Franklin School."

Mr. Boone thought every week at Franklin School was a special one. You had to like school a *lot* to be a principal. Cody hoped the special week wouldn't involve a reading contest, a spelling bee, a science fair, or something where you had to dress up and pretend you lived in the olden days.

"Next week," Mr. Boone said, "is our first-ever Franklin School pet show."

Cody could hardly believe his ears. The hubbub in the room showed that everyone else was excited, too. But nobody else could be as excited as Cody.

There would be prizes, Mr. Boone explained. For each grade level, a panel of pet experts would award the prizes for best animal in each species category, as well as a grand prize for best in show. There would also be a popularity prize voted on by students.

Cody's pets could win heaps and heaps! He

didn't like to raise his hand in class—that was the kind of thing Simon did all the time—but he had to ask. "How many pets can we enter?"

Mr. Boone grinned. "As many as you want!"

Two dogs. Two cats. Three chickens. One rooster. One pig. Cody counted on his fingers: nine!

"The point of the pet show is to raise money for the Humane Society," Mr. Boone said, pointing to his T-shirt. "So there will be an entrance fee for every pet you bring to school that day."

"How much?" someone else asked.

"Ten dollars," Mr. Boone replied.

Ten dollars?

Cody didn't have ten dollars. Last week he had gotten a twenty-dollar bill for his birthday, but he had already spent every penny of it on pet presents.

What was ten dollars times nine pets? Cody couldn't do tough math problems, like Annika

Riz, who was a math genius, but it had to be a fortune.

Cody would be lucky if he could come up with the money to enter *one* pet, let alone nine.

What kind of pet show would it be if Cody Harmon, king of pets, couldn't enter any pets at all?

2

After Mr. Boone headed off to spread the news of the pet show to the rest of the school, Mrs. Molina tried to get the class to settle down for math time.

"Boys and girls, get out your math books," she instructed.

Annika raised her hand. Probably she already had some hard math question Cody couldn't even understand.

"There should be *lots* of prizes in different categories," Annika said. "Like cutest pet, funniest pet, *smartest* pet."

Annika was always talking about her beagle, Prime, and the smart things he could do.

"It's math time now, Annika," Mrs. Molina reminded her, something she had certainly never needed to remind Annika of before.

Kelsey raised her hand next. Cody wondered what she would ask. Kelsey didn't care about math, and she didn't have any pets.

"I read a book once where there was a pet show, and there was a prize for the best costume," Kelsey said.

The class, mainly the girls, erupted into a din of oohs and aahs.

Cody was disgusted. That might be the worst idea he had ever heard. Pets hated costumes! He tried to imagine Sir B, his bantam rooster, in a costume but failed utterly.

"We're doing *math* now, Kelsey," Mrs. Molina said, sounding crosser this time.

Izzy Barr was now the third of the best-friend trio to have her hand in the air.

"Is this a question about *math*, Izzy?" Mrs. Molina asked.

"No, but—"

"This is *math time!*"

"But it's not fair! If we have a race, everyone can run. If we have a reading contest, everyone can read. But not everyone has a pet." Beneath her perky braids, Izzy's shoulders drooped.

Tobit leaned over and whispered to Cody, "Super Simon doesn't have a pet." Quite a few kids, including Simon, Tobit, Kelsey, and Izzy, had no pets at all.

The boys exchanged grins. There was finally one contest at Franklin School that Simon Ellis had no chance of winning!

"Boys and girls!" Mrs. Molina sounded as angry as Cody had ever heard her, which was saying a lot, as everyone knew she was the strictest teacher in the school. "I will pass on your comments—about pet categories, costumes, and fairness—to Mr. Boone. But right now, if you don't have your math books out and opened by the time I count to five, I'll . . ."

She trailed off as if trying to think of a fitting threat. Then her face softened.

"Given that this class can apparently think of nothing but the pet show," she said, "I'm going to change our plan for math time today."

Cody could tell from the glint in Mrs. Molina's eyes that he wasn't going to like the new plan for math time any better than the old one.

"I want each of you to come up with a word problem about pets."

Cody stifled a groan. Tobit groaned out loud.

Word problems were the *worst*.

If you were good at math but bad at writing, word problems were hard because they had writing in them.

If you were good at writing but bad at math, word problems were hard because they had math in them.

If you were bad at both, word problems were impossible.

Cody was bad at both.

"Then," Mrs. Molina finished, "I'll ask you to share your word problem with the class for everyone to solve. So put your math books away"— not that anyone but Simon had taken one out yet—"and see what creative, challenging word problems you can come up with about *pets*!"

Smiling broadly now, Mrs. Molina began passing out sheets of blank paper. Cody stared at his, trying to think of something to write. All around him, pencils scratched. Tobit grinned as he scribbled. He turned his paper so Cody could see what he had written:

If a dog poops and a cat poops and a bird poops, how much poop is there?

Cody cracked up.

"Boys!" Mrs. Molina warned them. Clearly she thought there was nothing to laugh about, or even smile about, in the whole of mathematics.

Finally it was time to share. Cody still hadn't written anything, and Mrs. Molina usually called first on whoever seemed worst prepared. But today she started with Simon.

"If Sally has ten dogs, and thirty percent of them are Dalmatians, twenty percent are Jack Russell terriers, twenty percent are corgis, and the rest are cocker spaniels, how many cocker spaniels does Sally have?"

For someone who had no pets, Simon sure knew the names of a lot of dog breeds. It would have taken Cody the rest of his life to answer that one, but Annika was already waving her hand in the air.

"Three!"

Cody stared at her.

"Annika, your turn," Mrs. Molina said.

"If Izzy gets a dog, and he runs at a speed of ten miles an hour, and he runs for fifteen minutes, how many miles has Izzy's dog run?" Izzy was the fastest runner in the class.

Simon had his hand in the air before she finished.

"Two point five. Or two and a half."

Cody stared harder. How could even Simon know that?

Kelsey read her problem next.

"Once upon a time"—talk about a dumb opening for a math problem—"there were three princesses named Kelselina, Izzabella, and Annikanna." She looked to see if her friends were beaming in appreciation of their new names. They were. "They lived together in a castle deep in a forest," Kelsey continued. "Although they were princesses, they were very poor. Kelselina's books were in tatters. Izzabella's slippers were worn through from her running. Annikanna's royal pet, her noble dog, Prime, had hardly any dog biscuits to eat."

Mrs. Molina asked, "Kelsey, is the word problem part of this coming soon?"

Kelsey sighed. "Okay. I'll skip the part about how they find the buried gold coins. But Kelselina finds three gold coins, and Izzabella finds four, and Annikanna finds five, so how many gold coins do they have?"

Cody could have answered that one, counting on his fingers, but he didn't feel like it.

"Twelve," someone called out.

"And then," Kelsey concluded, "they lived happily ever after."

Mrs. Molina adjusted her glasses. Cody could tell she was wondering if the pet word problems had been a bad idea after all.

She called on two more kids, not Cody or Tobit. Maybe she didn't want to hear the kind of word problem that would make two boys laugh out loud.

Cody's page was still blank, but if Mrs. Molina *had* called on him, he would have said: *If a boy has one pig, two dogs, two cats, one rooster, and three chickens, and it costs ten dollars to bring a pet to the pet show, and he doesn't have any money, how many pets can he bring?*

Even though he was bad at math, Cody knew the answer to that one all too well.

Zero.

At lunch recess, Cody and Tobit headed to the fence at the edge of the school field. It had been spray-painted with graffiti by some middle school kids on Halloween once and then painted over, but the big white letters spelling out *Boo* and *RIP* (for "rest in peace") still shone through. The letters made perfect targets for a throwing game, using stones from the gravel that edged the field.

Cody liked playing Boo-RIP, but even more he liked being outside, in the shade of the big oak tree, watching the squirrels dart about as they played. His favorite squirrel was a small one with a broken-off tail. Cody couldn't bear to think of how Stubby's tail might have gotten injured. But Stubby followed the others up and down the tree as well as if his tail were still long and bushy.

"*B!*" Cody called the letter as he aimed at the fence.

"*I!*" Tobit called his.

Both boys missed. Stubby watched from a safe distance.

As Cody hit the second *o* in *Boo* and Tobit missed the *P* in *RIP*, Cody asked Tobit, "Which pet should I bring for the pet show?"

As soon as he said it, he was sorry. He had too many pets to bring, but Tobit had no pets at all.

Sure enough, Tobit scowled. "Pet shows are dumb."

Cody wanted to say, *Pet shows are wonderful!*

But he didn't. And this pet show would be wonderful only if he could earn a lot of money to enter every single pet.

And earn it fast.

So he stopped talking about the pet show and concentrated on throwing his stones, pretending that he would get a dollar for each successful strike. By the time the bell sounded for the end of recess, he had earned eighteen dollars.

Too bad it was all in his head.

3

How can I earn some money?" Cody asked his mom after school as Rex padded after him into the kitchen.

Tibbie and Libbie had just gotten up from their afternoon nap. Tibbie was crawling toward Angus's bowl of kibble, which she had upset before school that morning. Libbie was crawling toward the cat door, which she had gotten her hand stuck in yesterday.

"Get Tibbie!" Cody's mother cried out as she dashed to snatch up Libbie.

Cody was already in pursuit.

The twins weren't identical. They were the other kind of twin, the kind that wasn't exactly the same. But they still looked a lot alike because they were both babies, and sisters, and born on the same day. Both had wisps of hair so blond it looked as if it wasn't there. Both had wide, determined smiles as they crawled toward their goals. And both could scream for a *long* time if you set them down when they wanted to be carried, or picked them up when they wanted to crawl.

Cody got to Tibbie just as Angus started growling at her to leave his kibble alone.

Angus was the second-biggest problem in Cody's life right now. First biggest: the pet show. Second biggest: a dog who ate homework—actually, who ate everything and then threw up afterward. And a dog who didn't like to share his food and toys with crawling babies.

"Cody," his mom said, "Angus is *your* dog. He needs to stop bothering the babies, or—"

Cody cut her off before she could finish saying that they'd have to find Angus another home. "The babies need to stop bothering him!"

His mother frowned. Cody knew who would get to stay in their house if his mother had to choose between Angus and the babies.

With both twins rescued and plopped into their side-by-side high chairs, Cody's mother said, "What were you asking?"

"How can I earn some money?" Cody replied.

Some kids, like Tobit, got an allowance. Their parents gave them money for doing nothing at all. Cody's parents gave him three dollars a week, but he had to clean out the cat boxes, fill food and water bowls, pick up dog poop from the yard, feed the chickens, and do whatever other farm chores his father asked him to do.

"How much money?" she asked, putting a few cut-up blueberries on each high-chair tray.

"Ten dollars." Well, ten dollars times nine. But he'd start by trying to earn ten. And actually, with the three dollars of allowance he'd get next week—he hoped he was doing the math right—only seven.

"You got twenty dollars for your birthday."

"I spent it."

She frowned.

"On stuff for the animals," he hastened to add.

"Well, then, I guess it's gone."

"Could you loan me the money? Just seven dollars, not ten?"

She shook her head, as he had known she would.

Tibbie was dropping her blueberries onto the floor. Libbie copied her. Angus gobbled up each one as it fell.

"There's a pet show at school," Cody explained. Maybe she'd loan him the money if she knew what it was for. "It costs ten dollars to enter. The money goes to the Humane Society."

She gave a sympathetic cluck. "What a shame you spent yours already," she said.

Thanks a lot, Mom.

Cody found his dad outside, mucking out the pen for Mr. Piggins. It was always easier to talk to his dad. He told his dad everything about the pet show, including how Mrs. Molina had informed the class that afternoon that Mr. Boone had said that pet costumes were a good idea, but he, Cody, thought they were a terrible idea.

Cody was sure Mr. Boone would bring a pet, and his pet would have the most amazing costume of all. Mr. Boone was more enthusiastic about school activities than everyone else in the school put together.

Cody's father chuckled. "How would you look in a costume, Piggins, my friend?" he asked the pig.

Ridiculous, was the answer.

"I asked Mom if she could loan me money, but she said no."

His dad scratched his chin. "I think I can find seven dollars' worth of work for you between now and the day of the pet show."

Cody's heart soared.

Then, just as quickly, it dropped back into his chest with a thud.

He'd be able to bring *one* pet, but *which* one?

Mr. Piggins was the biggest, and no one else at school had a pig. But Mr. Piggins had already been to school once, to be kissed by Mr. Boone at the end of the all-school reading contest. It seemed only fair to give another pet a turn.

Rex the golden retriever was the pet most likely to win a prize in a pet show, with his majestic head, silky fur, and model-dog behavior. Plus, even if it was wrong to love one pet more than the others, Cody loved Rex the best.

Angus was least likely to win, but maybe it would be good for Angus to get a special chance to shine. Maybe that would help Angus be a better-behaved dog, and Cody's mom wouldn't be mad at him all the time.

Then there were the cats. Puffball was so pretty, with her mottled coloring. And Furface was so affectionate, with her loud, deep purr.

His eyes fell on Sir B, the small rooster strutting around in the dirt. Cody doubted anyone at school had a rooster either. Sir B was so sure of himself; his feelings would be hurt if he was left behind.

The three chickens? They were just chickens, and they had each other for company. If he had to cross anyone off the pet show list, it would be the chickens. But the chickens didn't think of themselves as "just chickens." They deserved to go, too.

Still, taking one pet was better than taking none.

"What kind of work?" Cody asked. He'd do it cheerfully, whatever it was.

"I want you to do every bit of your homework, every day, the first thing when you get home from school. Your mother and I will check it, to make sure you've given it your best. And I don't want to hear any complaining."

Cody already felt like complaining. "Dad!"

But his dad gave him another grin. "Deal?"

Cody had no choice but to answer, "Deal."

Mr. Boone popped into Mrs. Molina's class the next day. Fortunately for Mrs. Molina, he arrived after math this time. If he had arrived before math, nobody, not even Annika and Simon, would have done a single math problem for the rest of the day.

For Mr. Boone had brought somebody else with him this time: a dog.

At first Cody didn't see the dog. All he heard were gasps of amazement from the kids nearest the classroom door. When Cody stood up from his chair to see what the fuss was about, there at the end of Mr. Boone's leash was the tiniest dog Cody had ever seen.

The itty-bitty Chihuahua must have weighed less than the five pounds that Libbie and Tibbie had each weighed at birth, but she proudly held up her head. It was covered with a Chihuahua-sized hat, and around her neck was tied a Chihuahua-sized bow.

Mrs. Molina sighed the way she always did when Mr. Boone came bounding into her room.

"What's happening here at school next week?" Mr. Boone asked the class.

"The pet show!" the class answered together.

"This little lady is not my own pet," Mr. Boone said sadly. Cody could see Izzy frowning in sympathy. "But I borrowed her from my next-door neighbor. I may borrow her again for the pet show. Unless I can borrow an elephant!"

Everyone laughed at the ridiculous thought of an elephant tromping into school.

"The pet show is going to finish up with a grand costume parade," Mr. Boone said.

Cody sighed.

"Do you like Bitsy's bonnet?"

Cheers came from everyone but Cody.

"Who wants to pet her?"

Every hand went up, including Cody's.

"I can't let everyone pet her, I'm afraid. That would be too much petting for this little dog. But . . ."

His eyes swept the room. Some kids were waving their hands so hard they were in danger of falling out of their chairs.

"Cody," he said. "Cody Harmon."

Now Cody almost fell out of *his* chair.

"How's your pig doing?" Mr. Boone asked him. "I bet you have the biggest pet of anyone in this room. So come meet the smallest."

All eyes on him, Cody left his seat, trying not to trip on his untied shoelaces as he made his way to the front of the room. He crouched down beside Bitsy, and the tiny dog, still on her leash, jumped up into his arms. Holding her close to his chest, he could feel the rapid beating of her heart.

"It's okay, Bitsy," he whispered to her. "There're a lot of kids here, but nobody will hurt you. You're a pretty girl." He hoped she wouldn't think he was complimenting her hat. "Not your hat," he added, "*you*."

Bitsy licked his hand.

If only dogs and cats and chickens and ferrets and hamsters and snakes and pigs could come to school every single day!

"All right, class," Mr. Boone said. "Bitsy and I have to be on our way. See you at the pet show! I'll be the fellow riding an elephant!"

Mr. Boone took Bitsy from Cody and was gone.

* * *

Tobit seemed in even a worse mood than yesterday as they played Boo-RIP at lunch.

"It's not that big a deal, you know," he said to
Cody.

What wasn't that big a deal?

"Petting a dog."

Was Tobit jealous of him? They were both so
used to being jealous of Simon that Cody could
hardly believe that anybody could ever be jealous of *him*.

"I didn't say it was," Cody said.

Tobit hurled his next stone so hard and care-
lessly that it soared over the top of the fence to
plunk down on the lawn on the other side.

"Do you want to play something else?" Cody
asked.

"It's boring just hitting stupid letters on a stupid fence," Tobit said.

"We could stand farther away, to make it

harder," Cody suggested, even though he knew that wasn't what Tobit was mad about.

"Or we could find a moving target," Tobit said, picking up another stone.

Before Cody had time to react, Tobit whirled around and threw it at one of the squirrels climbing up the tree.

It was Stubby.

Cody's heart clenched inside his chest. How could anyone throw a stone at a squirrel? Especially a squirrel with a broken tail?

Luckily Stubby scrabbled out of sight, hiding himself in the leaves starting to unfurl themselves on the branches.

"Don't!" Cody shouted as Tobit picked up another stone.

Tobit flushed a deep red. "I didn't even hit him!"

"But what if you had?"

"But I totally missed! Why are you making a big deal about *everything*?"

Luckily the bell rang before Cody could reply. And what would he have said? That he practically thought of Stubby as pet number ten? Tobit was already mad about anything to do with pets. Cody didn't want to make him any madder. So he dropped the last stone in his hand and headed back inside without saying anything more.

4

During silent reading time—which was anything but silent that day—Mrs. Molina called Cody's name. "Cody, I need to talk to you."

Tobit, standing next to Cody in the reading nook, both of them trying to take so long to pick out a book that reading time would be over before they found one, raised an eyebrow. Cody was glad Tobit was acting normal again after their near-quarrel during Boo-RIP.

But Cody had no idea what he had done wrong now. Try as he might, he couldn't think of a single thing.

When he made himself approach Mrs. Molina's desk, she was holding a stapled bunch of papers. Actually two pieces of paper, stapled to a messily written cover page.

His animal report.

Cody stood there, waiting to hear what Mrs. Molina was going to say.

"There is *poor* work," she began. "There is *disappointing* work. But then there is *unacceptable* work. Do you know what *unacceptable* means?"

Cody nodded.

"What does it mean?" she prompted.

Cody hated when grownups asked questions when they already had a specific answer in mind they wanted to hear, and you had to guess what you were supposed to say.

"I got an F on my animal report?" he asked.

He had gotten F's before, on spelling tests and math quizzes. His mom would yell, and his dad would be so nice about it Cody would feel even worse. But F's weren't the end of the world.

"No," Mrs. Molina said.

He had passed? Or maybe there was some grade even lower than F. F minus. Or G, a grade saved for a six-sentence report with zero sources.

Mrs. Molina went on. "*Unacceptable* means I cannot *accept* this."

She handed the report to Cody. He had no choice but to take it. Stapled to the back was an envelope addressed to his parents.

"Cody," Mrs. Molina said, "I'm giving you till a week from this Friday to do the report over again. This time the report will be three pages long. This time the report will have facts from two sources. This time you will print neatly and legibly. I'm giving you a second chance."

She smiled at him as if she had delivered good news instead of the worst news Cody had heard since he learned the pet show cost ten dollars per pet and costumes were expected.

"Yes, ma'am."

Cody's parents liked it when he said *sir* and *ma'am*. Besides, this seemed like a good time to be extra polite.

"I want you to bring the letter back tomorrow, signed by your parents."

"Yes, ma'am."

"All right. Go put your report in your backpack. I don't want you to lose it."

If only Cody could!

As Cody trudged to the coat cubbies, Tobit shot him an inquiring look.

"She's making me do my animal report over again!" Cody tried to keep his voice to a whisper.

"Wow," Tobit said, with genuine sympathy. "That's terrible." He made mad squinty eyes at Mrs. Molina, which fortunately she didn't see.

Cody was glad to have Tobit take his side, now that he was going to have to spend every day for the next week and a half writing three whole pages about pigs.

At home that afternoon Tibbie and Libbie crawled up to him as if they didn't know he had a horrible note to give his parents. Rex nuzzled the knees of Cody's pants. Angus nipped at his socks. The cats held back until the dogs had finished their greeting and then wrapped themselves around his legs.

"How was school?" his mother asked.

I got to hold a Chihuahua.

Tobit threw a stone at Stubby.

I have to do my animal report over again.

"It was okay," Cody said.

"Do you have any homework?"

"A little bit. Just some math and spelling."

And an entire animal report. He didn't want

to tell her yet. He'd tell his dad first, and his dad could help him tell his mom.

"Well, fix yourself a snack and get started," she said, snatching up Libbie as she was reaching to pull Angus's tail, and Tibbie as Angus was once again growling at her.

Just then Cody's dad came in, his face reddened by the spring sunshine, his thinning hair tousled by the spring breeze. His eyes crinkled into a smile when he saw Cody.

Cody might as well tell him now. He unzipped his backpack and produced his report with the attached note.

"Um . . . Mrs. Molina . . . well . . . she said . . . I have to . . ."

He handed the report to his dad. His mom, still clutching the babies, leaned over to look, too. Cody tried not to watch as his dad tore open the envelope and read whatever Mrs. Molina had written. He dropped down to the floor and busied himself stroking Rex's silky fur and trying to ignore Angus, who was back tugging at Cody's socks. If Angus were in Mrs. Molina's class, he'd get a note sent home every single day.

"Cody," his mom said, "I told you—"

His father cut her off. "Son," he said. "We made a deal. You know what you need to do."

Cody did. Seven dollars to enter one pet in the pet show if he did his homework without complaining. This was homework. Huge, horrible, hideous homework.

"Yes, sir," Cody told him.

"Let's make a plan," his dad said then. "Do you need to go to the library to get some books on pigs?"

Cody shook his head. "I brought home the two books I had in my desk at school."

"Great!" his dad said. "Just read one today and one tomorrow. I'll give you some index cards so that you can take notes, and more paper for writing your first draft."

Great?

Cody picked up his backpack and plodded up to his small room at the top of the stairs, where he had to spend the rest of a beautiful sunny afternoon reading.

There was a lot, it turned out, Cody hadn't known about pigs.

Pigs have forty-four teeth. Pigs have small lungs. Pigs roll around in the mud to keep cool. Pigs can run up to eleven miles in an hour.

It took Cody a long time to read the first pig book, even though it was a picture book for little kids. But the facts, he had to admit, were pretty cool. He wrote the best ones down on the index cards his dad had given him, the way Mrs. Molina had told the class to do.

That was all he needed to do on the report

today. Oh, and he had spelling and math, too. He looked out his bedroom window to where Rex was dozing in the afternoon sun and Angus was chasing one of the chickens, who fluttered to a safe perch atop a low stone wall.

"Angus, stop it!" Cody called out the window, not that Angus had ever listened to any human being about anything.

Angus looked up at him and wagged his tail, as if to say, *I wouldn't be chasing chickens if you came down to play with me.*

Why did Cody have to do spelling *and* math homework? Why was there such a thing as homework? Didn't teachers know a kid with nine pets didn't have time for homework?

But a deal was a deal.

Once Cody finally finished the rest of his homework and his mother had checked every single bit of it, he headed outside at last, a tennis ball in each hand. For the next half hour he

threw balls for the dogs, loving the sight of Rex dashing to find the ball however far he had thrown it. Angus dashed after every ball eagerly but only brought back half of them. He'd get distracted by a rabbit he needed to chase, or he'd forget which direction the ball had soared.

Cody would definitely bring Rex to the pet show, not Angus. Not the cats either. The cats were beautiful, but they didn't *do* as many things.

Unless he brought Mr. Piggins.

Rex or Mr. Piggins?

Mr. Piggins or Rex?

On Wednesday, Cody and Tobit had both brought their lunch, so they reached their usual table in the cafeteria ahead of the kids waiting in the food line.

Tobit took a big bite of his ham and cheese sandwich. "Izzy's right," he said. "The pet show's not fair to kids who don't have pets."

"Well," Cody said, "lots of things are unfair. Races are unfair to kids who are bad at running. Reading contests are unfair to kids who hate to read."

"Mr. Boone said he might borrow that little tiny dog for the pet show," Tobit went on.

Cody didn't like where this conversation was heading.

"So that means it's okay to borrow pets," Tobit continued.

Now Cody knew exactly what Tobit was going to say next.

"So I could borrow Rex!"

"No!" The word burst from Cody's lips before he had time to think of how to soften it. "I mean, I think I'm taking Rex."

"Or Mr. Piggins!" Tobit sounded even more excited now.

"I might take both of them," Cody said.

Tobit narrowed his eyes. "You don't have twenty dollars. I bet you don't even have ten."

"I'm working on earning it."

So far everything Cody had said was true, or sort of true, or might be true.

"Earning it, like how?"

"Doing stuff for my dad." It was too terrible to have to admit that the "stuff" he was doing was homework, homework, and more home-work.

"Well, you can't earn enough money to take all your pets," Tobit pointed out.

To Cody's relief, Jackson Myers and two other boys arrived with their trays, talking about their next soccer game on Saturday. All three boys had pets of their own. Jackson's pet was a ferret, which was definitely a cool pet, though not as cool as a pig or a rooster, and Ferrari the ferret was nowhere near as wonderful as Rex.

Was Cody a bad friend not to want Tobit to borrow Rex or Mr. Piggins? Or any pet? But how could he loan a pet to someone who would throw a stone at a poor little squirrel?

During afternoon recess, Cody was glad when Tobit headed over to the blacktop to play basketball with Jackson. He wanted to check the oak tree to see if Stubby was there and to try to decide what to do. He almost wished there wasn't going to be a pet show.

Izzy ran up and plopped down on the grass next to him. Cody liked Izzy best of the girls, and she liked him best of the boys, because they were the two fastest runners in the class.

"Hi," Izzy said.

"Hi," Cody replied.

"You look sad," Izzy said. "Are you?"

Cody was touched that Izzy cared enough to ask.

"Not really." He didn't want to tell her that Tobit was mad at him, or that he had too many pets and not enough money, or that he had to read another whole book about pigs as soon as he got home from school. So he said, "I wish the pet show didn't have costumes."

"Why?" Izzy asked. Before he could answer she said, "If you're not good at making costumes, we can make the costume for you!"

Cody didn't need to ask who *we* was. He already knew. Izzy, Annika, and Kelsey were always together.

"You're bringing Mr. Piggins, right?" Izzy asked.

"I'm not sure yet," Cody said.

"The three of us are great at costumes!" Izzy said. "Especially Kelsey, because she reads so much and gets lots of ideas from books. And Annika is already thinking of tons of costume ideas for her dog, Prime, so she's bound to have some leftover ones. And I want to meet your other pets. We can come this weekend! I have softball Saturday morning. So can we come on Saturday afternoon?"

It was all happening too fast. But it wasn't as if Cody had a single costume idea himself.

Izzy jumped up. "Tell Mr. Piggins help is on the way!"

5

Saturday morning Cody's soccer team won their game. Tobit scored the winning goal, which made Cody happy. Maybe Tobit would forget about trying to borrow one of Cody's pets.

Then, back at home, Cody spent a full hour copying animal facts from his note cards into sentences to put into his report, with his mother looking over his shoulder the whole time. He was grateful when the girls showed up at one.

Five minutes after they arrived, Kelsey already had Furface and Puffball in her lap.

"They're purring!" she marveled. "Does that mean they like me?"

"Sure," Cody said, even though both cats purred for anyone.

Annika was occupied with Rex. Cody could tell she was trying to find out if Rex was as smart as Prime.

"Sit!" she commanded.

Rex sat.

"Shake!"

Rex offered his paw.

"Lie down!"

Rex obeyed.

"Roll over!"

Rex rolled.

"But can he *count*?" Annika asked. "Prime can count. Well, almost count. Rex, bark once when I say the number one, and bark twice when I say the number two. Are you ready? Okay: two!"

No bark came from Rex.

"One!"

Silence from Rex.

Annika looked pleased, but Cody would have

bet the entrance fees for all of his pets put together that Prime couldn't really count either.

Izzy was already outside with Angus. She was the kind of girl who had a hard time sitting still. And Angus was the kind of dog that had a hard time sitting still. Through the window, Cody saw the two of them running around the yard side by side. Running and running and running.

"So," Kelsey said, "which pet needs a costume? Izzy said you were bringing Mr. Piggins? Or are you bringing the dogs and cats, too? Do you need one costume, or costumes for everyone?"

This was the moment of decision.

Cody wanted to bring Rex most. But Rex was the one who would most understand if he couldn't go. Rex was the one who understood everything. And nobody else at school had a pig.

"Mr. Piggins," Cody said, looking over at Rex, Furface, and Puffball with a guilty pang. And what about Sir B? And the chickens? Even awful Angus!

Kelsey looked sad, too, stroking a cat with each hand. "Will the others mind being left behind?"

"I don't have ten dollars for every single pet," Cody mumbled.

"That would be a lot of money," Annika agreed. "Two dogs, two cats, one pig: five times ten is fifty."

"No," Cody said. "I don't have five pets. I have *nine*." He told them about Sir B and the chickens.

"Ninety dollars," Annika corrected herself.

How could she do math like that so fast in her head?

Izzy came back inside, Angus bounding beside her, panting with joy. She threw herself down on the floor and Angus was all over her, licking her face, her hands, her bony knees, any part of her with skin to lick. Izzy couldn't stop giggling.

"Can I take Angus to the pet show?" Izzy pleaded. "Can I borrow him for just one day?"

Cody's stomach tightened. If only Mr. Boone hadn't told everybody that he had borrowed Bitsy! Izzy wasn't like Tobit. He didn't think she'd ever throw a stone at a broken-tailed squirrel. But it was strange and scary to think of any of his pets going off with anybody but him.

"That's what I was thinking!" Kelsey said. "If you let other kids borrow your pets, then *they'll* pay the ten dollars, and *all* your pets can go to the pet show, and the Humane Society can get . . ." She looked over at Annika. "How much money did you say it was?"

"Ninety dollars," Annika said.

"Ninety!" Kelsey proclaimed triumphantly. "Should I take Puffball or Furface?"

"Angus!" Izzy hugged the dog. "We're going to the pet show!"

"I'm taking my dog, Prime," Annika apologized to Rex. "But you're such a wonderful dog.

Somebody else will want to take you. Cody, Tobit doesn't have a pet, right? He can take Rex."

"No!" Cody said. He hadn't meant to say it so loudly.

"Tobit has a pet?" Kelsey asked.

"No, he doesn't, but . . ."

How could Cody say he didn't want to let his own best friend bring Rex to the pet show? But he didn't want to tell the girls about Stubby. He didn't want to make Tobit look bad in front of them.

Izzy was the only one who seemed to understand how scary it was to let other kids borrow his pets.

"I'll take good care of Angus," she promised. "Such good care! I'll be the best dog borrower there ever was!"

"I'll be the best cat borrower," Kelsey echoed. "If I can decide which cat to borrow."

Cody hadn't yet decided if anyone would get

to borrow any dog or cat. Or rooster. Or chicken. But apparently it had gotten decided for him. Ninety dollars would be a lot of money for the Humane Society. And this way every single pet would have a chance to shine.

"But . . ." He could already think of tons of problems with this plan. "What if everyone wants to borrow a pet? I only have nine. What if everyone wants to borrow the same one?"

What if Tobit still wants to borrow Rex?

The girls looked at one another, apparently stumped by the problem.

"You could draw names from a hat," Kelsey suggested slowly.

"But what if I don't get Angus?" Izzy moaned.

And what if Tobit got Rex?

"You could let people bid on them," Annika suggested. "The highest bidder wins, with the money going to the Humane Society. Think of how much you'd raise then!"

"But what if I can't afford Angus?" Izzy wailed.

And what if Tobit won the bid on Rex?

"You could have a sign-up sheet," Kelsey said. "Yes! First come, first served. And we came first, and it was our idea, so we get served first. But should I sign up for Furface or Puffball?"

"Yay!" Izzy shouted. "I get Angus!"

Cody sighed. Kelsey was already looking for a blank sheet of paper on the messy desk in the corner of the family room where his parents had the family's one ancient computer.

Three days ago Tobit had asked if he could borrow Rex. If this was first come, first served, Tobit was first.

But Tobit had thrown a stone at Stubby, even though the stone had missed.

"Here's some paper!" Kelsey crowed. "And here's a pencil, too. Okay. Mr. Piggins—Cody.

Angus—Izzy. Furface—me. Or Puffball—me? Or Furface—me? No, Puffball—Kelsey. Next: Rex. Everyone's going to want Rex. Who do you think will get to take him?"

The question made Cody's heart hurt.

6

He's big," Kelsey said as they all—including Rex and Angus—stood outside next to the pigpen. "I forgot how big he was."

"How much does he weigh?" Annika wanted to know.

"About five hundred pounds," Cody said proudly.

"Is that extra big?" Izzy interrupted her rough-housing with Angus to ask.

"No," Cody told her. "The biggest pig ever was almost two *thousand* pounds."

Who would have guessed a pig fact for his animal report would come in handy so soon?

"We're going to need a big costume," Kelsey pointed out. "A really big costume."

"I think it'd be funnier," Annika said, "if he had an itty-bitty costume. Or a tutu!"

"He's a *boy*," Cody reminded them.

"Piglet in *Winnie-the-Pooh* is a boy," Kelsey said. "He wears this little striped outfit. But it covers most of him. So I don't think Mr. Piggins can dress up as Piglet. Wait! Wilbur in *Charlotte's Web*! No. He doesn't wear any clothes."

Cody started getting his hopes up. "So maybe Mr. Piggins doesn't need clothes either?"

"Cody," Kelsey said, "that's why we're *here*. To come up with a costume for him." She closed her eyes, as if trying to remember the pictures from the book. "Wilbur does win a blue ribbon at the fair. So we could put a blue ribbon on Mr. Piggins—or a sash! Yes, a big blue sash that says SOME PIG, TERRIFIC, and RADIANT. Those are things Charlotte weaves about him in her web. And we can put a toy spider on his head!"

"Nobody but you will get it," Cody said.

"Everyone will totally get it!" Kelsey protested.

"Cody's right," Izzy chimed in. Cody had thought she was too busy tumbling on the ground with Angus to be listening.

"Well," Annika said, "everyone will think Mr. Piggins is so amazing that his costume doesn't really matter."

Cody's thoughts exactly.

"So can we make him be Wilbur?" Kelsey begged. "I'll make the sash, and I have a little stuffed spider."

Annika nodded. Izzy, rolling on the grass with Angus, flashed a grin.

Cody shrugged. "Fine."

Mr. Piggins's costume was the least of his worries right now.

After the girls had gone, Cody knew he should work some more on his animal report. It would be terrible if after all the time he had spent on it so far, he didn't end up doing a good enough job to earn Mr. Piggins's entry fee. But instead he sat staring at the list Kelsey had started.

Mr. Piggins	Cody Harmon
Angus	Izzy Barr
Puffball	Kelsey Green
Furface	?
Rex	?
Sir B	?
Chicklet	?
Daisy	?
Doodle	?

Rex nuzzled his nose against Cody's leg.

"Maybe I should take you and let someone else take Mr. Piggins," Cody said aloud.

Rex looked up at him with his beautiful brown eyes.

But who else had a kindhearted dad with a

pickup truck who would be willing to haul a five-hundred-pound pig to school? Plus, Kelsey had her heart set on making the Wilbur costume.

"Whoever gets you has to be worthy of you," Cody said to Rex. "He can't be the kind of person who would throw a stone at a squirrel even if the stone missed. You're a perfect dog. You need to be with a perfect human."

Rex gave his tail an approving thump. Cody knew Rex wasn't bragging about how perfect he was. Rex thumped his tail because he approved of anything Cody said. Rex and Cody agreed on everything.

The only thing Cody hated even more than doing homework was talking on the phone, even to people he loved, like his Grandma Jean and Grandpa Joe. It was always a terrible moment when his mother would be on the phone talking to them, and she'd say, "Oh, Cody's right here.

I'll let him say hello to you." And then he could never think of a single word to say.

But now he found the Franklin School directory his mother kept in the drawer of the desk in the family room and looked up the number he wanted.

The person who answered was a woman who sounded like a mother. This was getting harder by the minute.

"Is . . ." Cody made himself keep going. "Is Simon there?"

"May I tell him who's calling?"

What was that supposed to mean? Then Cody figured it out: this was a weird way of asking his name.

"Sure. I mean, it's Cody. Cody Harmon. From school."

A moment later he heard Simon's voice. "Hello?"

"You don't have a pet, right?" Cody asked.

"No," Simon said, sounding bewildered by the question. Maybe Cody should have found some way to lead up to it.

"Do you want to have one?"

"Not really." Simon sounded even more bewildered. "I don't think I'd have time for one, because of homework and violin. Pets are a big responsibility."

"I mean, would you like to borrow my dog for the pet show? You'd have to pay the ten dollars for his entry fee and make him a costume—not a dumb costume, but a costume that wouldn't make him look ridiculous, because I don't want anybody laughing at him. And you'd have to take good care of him, extra good care of him, during the show."

"I could do those things," Simon said. He paused. "But . . . why?"

Cody told him about his problem of too many pets, and not enough money to enter them, and the plan the girls had helped him make.

"I'll bring the sign-up sheet to school on Monday," Cody said. "But Rex is my golden retriever, and he's not an ordinary dog. So I didn't want him going to whatever kid grabbed the sheet first. He's actually the best dog in the entire world."

"Wow," Simon said.

Cody tried to decide if Simon was being sarcastic. But Simon wasn't a sarcastic kind of person. He was a serious kind of person who got straight A's and was the best at reading, the best at math, the best at spelling, the best at everything.

"I'll do my best," Simon said.

Cody felt as if a giant had stooped down and lifted off the heavy stone crushing his heart.

"Can I meet Rex first?" Simon asked. "So he'll feel comfortable with me at school that day? And so I can get an idea for a costume that will fit his personality?"

"Definitely!"

But as soon as Cody hung up, the humongous stone dropped back onto his chest with a thud.

What was Tobit going to say when he found out Cody hadn't loaned Rex to him, but had loaned him to Super-Duper-Pooper Simon?

7

Even worse than doing homework *or* talking on the phone, Cody remembered too late on Monday morning, was talking to Mrs. Molina. But he had to tell her about the pet sign-up sheet.

Luckily, as he was trying to summon up his nerve before morning announcements, the three girls snatched the piece of paper from on top of his pile of books and hurried to Mrs. Molina's desk. Cody jumped up from his seat and followed them.

Kelsey did most of the explaining, with Annika chiming in with how much money they'd raise for the Humane Society if all of Cody's pets could come.

"And I'm bringing Angus!" Izzy finished.

Cody waited for Mrs. Molina to adjust her glasses. He waited for her to ask him how he could be spending so much time on the pet show when he was supposed to be redoing his unacceptable animal report.

Instead she gave him a big smile.

"What a generous idea, Cody!"

Even though it hadn't been his idea and he hadn't even liked it at first, he felt himself grinning. After all, he was the only kid in the class who had nine pets. The plan couldn't have happened without him.

After the pledge and announcements, Mrs. Molina called the class to attention.

"Boys and girls," she announced, "some of you have complained you don't have a pet to bring to the pet show. Well, Cody has been kind enough to offer to loan out some of his. Before you volunteer, know that if you borrow one of Cody's pets, you will have to pay its entrance fee. And you'll be fully responsible for following the pet show rules that day."

Mrs. Molina squinted at Cody's list. He had added the type of animal each pet was. People needed to know that Furface was a cat, and the other two were a rooster and three chickens.

"My!" Mrs. Molina said. "Some of Cody's pets are quite unusual. One of them is a cat, but—"

"I want Rex!" Tobit called out.

Cody stared down at his desk. He couldn't let himself meet Tobit's eyes.

"I don't believe Rex is available," Mrs. Molina said, studying the list again.

"Then I want Angus!" Tobit shouted, again without raising his hand.

"The available pets," Mrs. Molina said, ignoring Tobit's outburst, "are a cat named Furface, a rooster named Sir B, and three chickens named Chicklet, Daisy, and Doodle. How many of you are interested in borrowing a pet?"

Cody couldn't resist glancing around to scan the room. Half a dozen hands were in the air, including Tobit's.

"We're not going to have a stampede," Mrs. Molina said, clearly addressing the comment to Tobit. "I'll write each of your names on a slip of paper, and Cody will draw them out of a hat. Cody, go get your baseball cap."

On his way to the coat rack to retrieve his cap from its hook, Cody counted the hands again. Exactly six hands were raised, for the five remaining pets. He already felt sorry for the kid who would be the only one left out. But he still hoped it would be Tobit.

Some friend I am, he accused himself bitterly.

"All right, Cody, let's get this done," Mrs. Molina said, eyeing the clock, with math time approaching. "Call out the names one by one, and each person in turn will choose which pet to borrow for the pet show."

Cody closed his eyes and reached his hand into the hat for the first slip of paper.

Elise, a quiet girl who liked to draw, chose Furface.

Tanner, a boy on Cody's soccer team, chose Chicklet. That surprised Cody. He would have thought a boy would pick a rooster. Maybe Tanner liked the name Chicklet. Cody had been pleased with himself when he thought of it.

He plunged his hand for the third time into the hat. This time the slip, in Mrs. Molina's extremely neat printing, said Tobit.

Should Cody pretend it said Hazel, Millie, or Jake? Nobody else could see it but him.

No. Cody didn't cheat.

"Tobit," he read.

"The rooster!" Tobit shouted, as if he had wanted Sir B all along. *Tobit had better take good care of Sir B*, Cody thought. But with his

fierce beak and claws, Sir B was pretty good at taking care of himself.

Jake chose Doodle. Hazel and Millie decided to share Daisy.

"Now everyone who wanted one has a pet to bring to the show," Mrs. Molina concluded. "Thank you, Cody!"

The class clapped.

To make the moment even sweeter, Mr. Boone came in as Cody was hanging his cap back on his hook. Today the principal was carrying a rabbit that was wearing a rabbit-sized Franklin School T-shirt and a Franklin School baseball cap with two holes cut in it for the rabbit's droopy ears to poke through.

"Ooh!" the class squealed.

Even Cody didn't think this costume was dumb. Okay, it was dumb, but it was also so cute that Cody joined in the oohs and aahs of the rest of the class. If only he could have just one more pet, he'd want it to be a rabbit with droopy ears, white fur, and a twitching pink nose.

"This is Bunnikin," Mr. Boone said. "Come on up—quietly—to say hello."

The class surged forward on tiptoe, but Mr. Boone didn't let anyone hold Bunnikin the way he had let Cody hold Bitsy.

"Is this the pet you're bringing to the pet show?" one kid asked.

"Maybe," Mr. Boone said. "If my elephant doesn't arrive in time."

He winked at the class and headed off, Bunnikin's ears bobbing.

Cody didn't sit at his usual table at lunch, afraid of questions from Tobit. Carrying his tray, he snuck over to a table filled with second graders. Tobit found him there anyway.

"Who's taking Rex?" Tobit demanded. So much for the hope that Tobit wouldn't be mad.

There was no point in lying. Tobit was going to find out sooner or later. Avoiding Tobit's eyes, Cody muttered in a voice so low he hoped Tobit wouldn't hear it, "Simon."

"Simon?" Tobit practically shouted. "Simon?!"

Cody couldn't think of an explanation that wouldn't make Tobit even madder. How could he tell Tobit he had actually called Simon on the phone and asked him to take Rex? How could he tell Tobit he hadn't been able to bear the thought that his own closest friend would borrow the pet Cody loved best?

The answer was simple: he couldn't.

Cody wanted to say, *You shouldn't have thrown that stone at Stubby.*

But he didn't know how to say that either.

Besides, Tobit had already stomped over to their third-grade table, without looking back.

8

Loaning your pets for a pet show, Cody was finding out, was a lot of work. And a lot of worry.

Cody couldn't just let the pet borrowers come and collect their pets. The cats weren't going to want to sleep at strange houses. Cats like the comfort of being at home. In fact, Cody was starting to think the cats weren't going to like the pet show. At least Furface and Puffball were friendly cats, who enjoyed rubbing themselves on everyone's ankles. But there would be so many ankles at the pet show.

The chickens couldn't stay with strangers

either. They couldn't sleep inside houses because they were too messy. They couldn't sleep outside houses because a fox might eat them. They needed to sleep in their own safe, familiar coop.

Angus, however, was going to spend the night before the pet show having a sleepover with Izzy. Izzy had begged, and Cody had said yes. But he was going to have to remember to pack Angus's dog food, leash, and squeak toys.

Rex *could* stay the night with Simon. But Cody didn't want him to.

This meant on the pet show day, Cody and his dad would have to transport one dog, two cats, three chickens, one rooster, and one five-hundred-pound pig to school, all in crates or carriers, except for Rex, who could be on his leash.

Some dads might not want to take off a whole morning from work to haul a pickup truck full of animals. But when Cody had asked his dad, all his dad did was give his slow grin and say, "Sure, son, I think I can manage it." Then he'd added, "*If* a certain animal report is completed."

"It will be!" Cody promised. He had two whole pages written. He needed just one more.

It was hard writing that last page, though, with a parade of kids coming by to meet their pets and plan their costumes.

After school on Tuesday, Simon came to meet Rex.

After school on Wednesday, Elise came to meet Furface.

After school on Thursday, Tanner, Jake, Hazel, and Millie came to meet the chickens.

After school every single day Izzy came to play with Angus. Each time she left, the little terrier kept running to the door at any sound, hoping it was Izzy coming back to play again.

The only pet borrower who didn't come was Tobit. Of course, Tobit already knew Sir B. But he didn't seem to have much interest in figuring out Sir B's costume. The boys still sat at their same lunch table, and they still went to soccer practice on Tuesday evening, but they didn't talk directly to each other. Cody hardly had time to mind, with Elise asking him if he thought Furface would look beautiful in a tiara and jeweled collar, and Hazel and Millie asking him if he knew where to find a blond wig to fit a chicken.

Still, it was strange to go out to recess each day and not play Boo-RIP.

When Cody finally finished his report the night before the pet show, it was three pages, though he had to write big on the last page to fill it to the bottom. He even had a special page called the bibliography, where he listed the two books he had read. His best pig facts had come from the first book he read, so one book would have been plenty. But he had two anyway.

He found his parents in the family room. Even with one dog, two cats, and two crawling, laughing, crying babies, the house was quieter than it had been for as long as Cody could remember. Cody hadn't realized that Angus made more noise and got into more trouble than the other eight of his pets put together. With Angus off on his sleepover, nobody ate anything disgusting and threw it up on the carpet. Nobody growled at the babies.

"I finished my report," Cody said, holding it out to his father.

He calmed his nerves by stooping down to stroke Rex's soft fur. His parents set the babies on the floor to play and then settled back on the couch and began reading.

"Is it . . . . okay?" Cody finally asked when they looked up from the last page.

"It's more than okay," his mother said, standing to give him a hug. "It's wonderful!"

Grinning, his father pulled his worn wallet from his back pocket and produced a five-dollar bill and two crinkled ones.

"You earned that seven dollars, son," he said.

Outside, in the falling light of the spring evening, Cody washed Mr. Piggins and polished his hooves. Kelsey had promised to bring the sash and spider to school tomorrow. Mr. Piggins would be the biggest pet there—unless Mr. Boone really did show up on an elephant.

If he did, that would be so cool!

Maybe he'd let Cody ride on the elephant, the way he had let Cody hold Bitsy.

Before Cody fell asleep, he pictured himself sitting astride an elephant's broad back, swaying from side to side as the elephant swung its long trunk back and forth, back and forth . . .

Even Cody's mother helped transport the pets to school the next morning. With the twins side by side in their matching car seats, she drove Cody, Rex, and the cats (in matching carriers) in her car. His dad loaded Mr. Piggins and the poultry into the back of his pickup and followed.

The first thing Cody saw when he got out of the car was an elephant holding up a stop sign and helping kids cross the street in front of Franklin School.

It wasn't a real elephant, of course. It was standing on two legs and directing traffic. It had to be Mr. Boone dressed in a very realistic elephant costume.

Cody couldn't help feeling disappointed. He had really thought Mr. Boone might be directing traffic atop the massive back of an actual elephant. But maybe even Mr. Boone couldn't find a real elephant, in the middle of Colorado, to borrow for the pet show.

The fake elephant waved at Cody, who was now holding Rex by his leash.

Cody waved back. Most schools didn't have a principal who would wear an elephant costume to school. A principal in an elephant costume was still better than no elephant at all.

Cody's mother couldn't leave the babies alone in the car, so she waited with Puffball and Fur-face for Cody to bring Kelsey and Elise out to retrieve them.

Inside the school, all was chaos. The third-grade part of the pet show was the first one of the day (Mrs. Molina had probably wanted to get it over soonest), so the third graders, their parents, and their pets streamed toward the gym.

After Cody dropped his backpack in Mrs. Molina's room, he and Rex followed everyone else to the gym, where Cody paid his ten dollars for Mr. Piggins while Rex sat quietly at his side. Cody was willing to bet no other third graders had worked as hard for their entrance fee as he had.

Simon met Cody at the check-in table and

took Rex's leash. Cody's heart tugged as Rex followed Simon into the area marked Dogs with a large sign.

Don't start loving Simon more than you love me!

Izzy was already there with Angus, who was being surprisingly good, not straining at the leash to get into a huge happy dog fight with his fellow contestants. Izzy was bouncing up and down with excitement, her short tight braids bobbing like a bunny's ears.

Kelsey and Elise followed Cody back to his mom's car to collect Puffball and Furface and then take them to the library, where cats were going to be judged.

"Have a wonderful time at the pet show!" Cody's mom told him before she drove away with the twins, who were too little to join the pet show audience. "And don't forget to give your report to Mrs. Molina!"

The chickens and Sir B, still in their crates, were outside with his dad. Through the open gym door, Cody could see Tanner, Jake, Hazel, and Millie, who were holding poultry costumes, talking to his dad, and admiring Mr. Piggins. No pets were in costume yet. The contest rules said the pets wouldn't wear their costumes until the grand parade at the very end.

Where was Tobit? Tobit had more tardies than anyone else in their class, but Cody couldn't believe anyone would be late on pet show day. Maybe Tobit was sick? Cody felt half relieved that he wouldn't have to worry about Tobit doing something mean to Sir B, and half sad that Sir B wouldn't get his chance to compete in the pet show with the rest.

A strange thought occurred to Cody. Right now, he, the kid with the most pets of anybody, was there in the gym without a single one.

The three judges—two women and one

man—were in place at a table set up to the side in the gym. Cody was glad to see that one of the women was Dr. Suh, his vet—well, his pets' vet. She gave him a big smile from across the room. The other two judges were the man who owned the Plenty of Pets store and the woman who was the head of the Humane Society.

Surely three people who knew so much about pets would know one of Cody's pets deserved the prize for best in show.

Cody loved all of his pets. But he was rooting most for Rex. And if Tobit didn't arrive soon, he couldn't root for Sir B at all.

Then he saw Tobit come in, carrying what appeared to be a rooster costume made out of tinfoil.

Was Cody glad to see his friend or not? He really didn't know.

9

With Mr. Piggins waiting outside with his dad in the truck, Cody had time to watch the judging of the other pets.

The judges came as a team to inspect fish in bowls, rabbits and guinea pigs and hamsters in cages, and a snake in its terrarium. They visited the chickens and Sir B in their crates. There was a brief scuffle as Jackson's ferret, Ferrari, darted away from Jackson and made a mad dash across the gym. Jackson, a fast runner on their soccer team, caught Ferrari a moment later.

Cat judging took place in the library. Puffball

seemed happy enough to be cuddling with Kelsey. Furface purred in the arms of Elise.

During the dog judging, each dog walked on a leash past the judges' table. Izzy's face glowed with pride as she led Angus, who pranced along beside her as happily as if he didn't belong to a boy named Cody. Rex was so regal and beautiful, his eyes the wisest and kindest, his fur the softest, his gait the most noble. Simon handled him as expertly as if Rex were his own dog.

Didn't his pets miss Cody even a little bit?

Finally it was Cody's turn to lead the judges outside to behold Mr. Piggins, who had come down the ramp from the truck and was waiting patiently on the grass with Cody's dad.

"What a fine fellow he is!" exclaimed Dr. Suh as she ran her hand along the pig's huge haunches.

"How much does he weigh?" marveled the pet shop man, who had certainly never had a pet this big in his store.

"He's lucky to be so well cared for," the Humane Society lady said.

Cody felt himself beaming.

"You're the boy with all the pets, right?" she asked then.

Cody nodded.

"Mr. Boone told us about you. Thanks for letting your friends borrow your pets today, and raising so much money for the shelter," she told him.

That almost made up for the fact that his pets hardly felt like *his* pets right now.

The last event of the pet show was the costume parade. In the gym and the library, kids and their parents were busy dressing up pets. Not all the pets were participating in the parade. Pets in the parade had to be able to walk on a leash or be carried securely by their owner or borrower. Otherwise it wouldn't be a *parade.*

Cody placed Kelsey's blue sash on Mr. Piggins: SOME PIG! TERRIFIC! RADIANT! These things were as true of Mr. Piggins as they were of the pig in the book Kelsey kept talking about. Cody taped the small stuffed spider onto Mr. Piggins's head. The pig didn't seem to know or care he had a spider perching there.

Then Cody led Mr. Piggins, on his halter, into the gym, to cheers from the third graders from all three classes.

In that moment Cody felt sorry for all the kids in the school, and in the world, who didn't have a pig.

His eyes found Rex, wearing the perfect costume: a simple white shirt collar and plaid bow tie that made him look like a distinguished gentleman and not a bit ridiculous.

Angus, however, looked completely ridiculous. Izzy had dressed him up as a plate—well, a heap—of spaghetti (tangled orange yarn) and meatballs (brown-dyed tennis balls, stuck all over him). She was laughing so hard she could hardly jog along beside him. Angus kept trying to tug at the meatball nearest his mouth, which made the whole thing even funnier.

Annika's beagle, Prime, wore a superhero cape covered with math equations like $2+2=4$. But just because a dog wore a math cape didn't mean the dog could *do* math.

Cody saw Kelsey and Puffball, both in costume. Kelsey wore a red cloak with a hood and carried a small cloth-covered basket. The cat wore an old-lady cap and wire-rimmed glasses. Oh. Little Red Riding Hood and her grandmother! Cody got it now.

Furface was decked out in a tiara and jewels. Maybe Cody should change her name to Princess Furface.

Chicklet wore a necklace made of Chicklets.

Daisy wore a wreath of fake daisies.

Doodle wore a tiny polka-dot birthday party hat.

Cody was surprised how well the chickens

walked with their string leashes tied around their necks.

Then he saw Tobit dragging Sir B, who did not look pleased in a tinfoil contraption that appeared to have been thrown together that morning. Cody had no idea what it was supposed to be, or if it was even supposed to be anything. Tobit laughed as if it was funny that Sir B was so mad. This wasn't like Izzy's gale of giggles at Angus's spaghetti-and-meatballs costume. Roosters don't like being led around by someone else; roosters like to be the ones doing the leading.

Then—it happened so fast—Cody couldn't tell if Sir B yanked loose from Tobit's grip or if Tobit let him go on purpose for the fun of seeing what would happen next.

What happened next was an enraged rooster flapping himself fiercely toward other kids' dogs, cats, and ankles and shaking off pieces of

tinfoil everywhere. That set off a din of barking and caterwauling. Angus's bark was loudest.

Cody let go of Mr. Piggins's halter. The pig had enough sense to stand still. Pigs are not easily flustered.

He darted up to Sir B, grabbed him, and covered him in one quick motion with some kid's sweatshirt that had been dropped onto the gym floor. He could feel the agitated rooster calm down in the comforting darkness. Then he carried Sir B over to his dad.

See?! Cody felt like shouting to his classmates. *Pet costumes are dumb! And pet costume parades are even dumber!*

But he was maddest at Tobit, who stood there in the middle of the gym floor still laughing.

10

With order finally restored and all the pets back in their places, Mr. Boone, no longer in his elephant costume, came to the microphone on the judges' table.

"The time has come," Mr. Boone said, "to announce the prizes."

Cody could see the teachers busy counting the slips of paper kids had dropped into the ballot box for the popularity prize. The only rule was that you couldn't vote for your own pet.

"Best snake," Mr. Boone read from the judges' list, "Jake. Exhibited by Tara Ling." The kids in

Mrs. Rodriguez-Haramia's class cheered extra loud.

He called out best hamster, best guinea pig, best fish, best hermit crab (Cody had missed seeing that one), best rabbit, and best ferret (Jackson's Ferrari).

"Best rooster: Sir B. Exhibited by Tobit Johnson."

Of course, Sir B was the only rooster. But the rules didn't say that there had to be more than one pet in each category. Jake the snake had been the only snake. And Sir B hadn't been a particularly well-behaved rooster. But he wouldn't have gotten loose if it hadn't been for Tobit.

"Best chicken." Who would it be? Cody divided his heart into thirds, rooting for each chicken equally. "Daisy," Mr. Boone read. Millie and Hazel hugged each other.

"Best pig: Mr. Piggins. Exhibited by Cody Harmon." The cheers from the whole gym made

Cody think Mr. Piggins had a good chance at the popularity prize.

"Best cat." Furface! Puffball! But the prize went to a cat belonging to a girl in Mr. Knox's class.

Then the final species prize.

"Best dog." It had to be Rex! It just had to be. "Rex. Exhibited by Simon Ellis."

Hooray!

"And now," Mr. Boone said, "best in show." That meant the best pet in all the categories put together, the best pet in the whole entire third grade at Franklin School.

To add drama, Mr. Boone rapped out a drumbeat on the judges' table.

"The prize for best of show goes to . . . Rex! Exhibited by Simon Ellis."

Cody's eyes brimmed with tears of pride. Rex, *exhibited* by Simon Ellis, but *loved* by Cody Harmon. Kids who didn't know any better were congratulating Simon. Cody didn't mind. Rex was his dog, his dog forever.

"Last but not least," Mr. Boone said, looking at the paper handed him by Mrs. Molina. "The popularity prize goes to . . ." He beat another drumroll on the table. But he didn't even need to announce the name because some kid started the chant, and other students took it up: "Mister Pig-gins! Mis-ter Pig-gins!"

Mr. Boone held up his hand to silence them.

"The prize goes to . . . I'm not sure I can read the handwriting here." Cody could tell he was joking; teachers had extremely excellent printing *and* cursive. "The first word starts with an *M*, and then there's a second word. I think it starts with a *D*? No, a *P*. Wait . . . Okay, I think I can read it now. The popularity prize goes to Mr. Piggins, exhibited by Cody Harmon."

More cheers rocked the gym.

The proudest hour of Cody's life was over.

* * *

On his way back to Mrs. Molina's room, with the pets safely loaded into his dad's pickup, Cody found Tobit blocking his path.

"Why?" Tobit demanded, as if he were a troll demanding payment before he would let Cody pass.

"Why what?" Cody asked, even though he could guess what Tobit was asking.

"*I* wanted to take Rex, and you let *Simon* take him, and then Simon got best dog *and* best in show, which is like winning best of *everything*, when he already wins best of everything *all the time*! I'm your best friend, and you let Super-Duper-*Pooper* Simon take Rex?"

Everything Tobit had said was true.

What Cody said next was true, too. "You shouldn't have thrown that stone at Stubby."

Tobit looked blank, as if he had no idea what Cody was talking about.

"The *stone*?" Cody prompted. "When we were

playing Boo-RIP? That you threw at *Stubby*? The squirrel?"

Comprehension dawned on Tobit's face. Then he flushed pink with rage.

"*That's* why you wouldn't let me take Rex? Because of a dumb *squirrel*? A dumb squirrel that doesn't even have a *tail*?"

"He's not dumb! And he can't help his tail! And I did let you take Sir B anyway, and you let Sir B get loose on purpose, I know you did."

"Didn't you think it was funny?" Tobit asked. "Come on, it *was*."

"It wasn't funny! Pets might have gotten hurt. Sir B might have gotten hurt."

Tobit shoved Cody, hard.

Cody shoved back, harder.

Suddenly Mr. Boone was there, with a hand on each boy's shoulder.

"Boys," he said sorrowfully, "what's this about? Maybe we'd better go into my office and work things out."

The next thing Cody knew, he was sitting in one of the chairs facing Mr. Boone's large cluttered desk, with Tobit there beside him. Cody had never been in the principal's office before. He had expected it to be a scary place, sort of like a jail for bad kids. But this office felt friendly. The overstuffed armchairs were cozy. There was a big jar of M&M's on Mr. Boone's desk, with a little spigot you could turn to release a few into your hand.

"Have some," Mr. Boone told them, pointing to the M&M's. "I might have some myself." He took a generous handful and popped them into his mouth in one big gulp.

Cody shook his head in response to the principal's invitation. He was too upset at Tobit to feel like nibbling on candy. Tobit didn't take any either.

"So," Mr. Boone said then, "what's going on?"

"He wouldn't let me borrow Rex!" Tobit burst out. "He let Simon have him instead!"

"He threw a stone at Stubby!" Cody shot back. "And he let Sir B loose on purpose!"

After both boys had a chance to explain, Mr. Boone didn't say anything for a long time. Then he said, "Do you want to know why I didn't ride an elephant to school today?"

The question was so surprising that Cody stole a glance at Tobit to see if Tobit looked puzzled, too. He did.

Both boys shook their heads.

"I *wanted* to ride an elephant," Mr. Boone said. "Ever since I was your age, I've wanted to ride an elephant."

Cody tried to picture Mr. Boone as a chubby, bald nine-year-old boy. He couldn't do it.

"So I looked for an elephant to borrow for today. And I found one, at a small local company that rents out exotic pets—elephants, giraffes, gorillas—for birthday parties. But when I went there to reserve my elephant, I couldn't do it."

"Why?" Cody asked.

"It was too sad." The principal had tears in his eyes, remembering. "That huge majestic beast . . . in this cramped cage. It should have been free in the wild, but it was being hired out for entertainment, to be ridden into an elementary school by a fellow like me. I couldn't go through with it."

Tears stung Cody's eyes, too.

"So," Mr. Boone said, "you may be wondering what this has to do with dogs, squirrels, and roosters."

Cody did.

"I'm saying, Cody, that I understand why you were upset that someone would hurt a squirrel and tease a rooster. And, Tobit, I'm saying that I didn't realize at first that my elephant plan was a bad idea. I was ready to treat an animal in a way that wasn't kind because I didn't *know* how bad it would make the elephant feel."

Cody waited to see if Mr. Boone would say anything else.

But all he said was, "Okay, boys, have some M&M's."

Cody took a handful. Tobit did, too.

"And now I need to get to the second-grade part of the pet show. I heard one girl there has a pet tarantula!"

11

When Cody and Tobit returned to Mrs. Molina's class, math time was under way. Cody handed her their pass from Mr. Boone, took his seat, and opened his math book. Even on the day of the pet show, Mrs. Molina's class still did math. If a tornado were to hit the school, Cody was sure Mrs. Molina's class would be doing math in the tornado shelter. If an earthquake struck, Mrs. Molina's class would do math amid the rubble.

After math came silent reading.

"Cody," Mrs. Molina called as the students were opening their books. "Come here, please."

Did Mrs. Molina know that he and Tobit had been shoving each other in the hall? He was pretty sure she wouldn't deal with boys who had been fighting by telling stories about an elephant.

Cody walked slowly to her desk.

"Cody," she said, "thank you for sharing your pets with your classmates so that everyone would be able to participate today. And congratulations on getting pet show prizes for so many of them!"

He let out his breath with relief.

"But, Cody"—this was starting to sound more like regular Mrs. Molina—"I gave you until today to present me with an acceptable animal report. Do you have it with you?"

Despite his mother's reminder, Cody had completely forgotten to turn it in.

"It's in my backpack!"

He raced to the coat cubby, unzipped his backpack, grabbed his report, and thrust it—three pages plus bibliography—into Mrs. Molina's hands. She read through it, page after page, as he stood there waiting.

"Cody," she said once she had finished, "what have you learned here?"

He wasn't sure what he was supposed to say. He had certainly learned a lot of facts about pigs.

Mrs. Molina answered for him. "You learned that you can write a fine report if you put your mind to it."

And then she smiled.

Outside at lunch recess, Cody saw Izzy, Kelsey, and Annika huddled together on a bench at the edge of the playground.

He looked more closely.

Izzy was crying. Kelsey had her arm around Izzy's shoulders. Annika knelt down in front of her, patting Izzy's knee.

It was none of Cody's business why Izzy was crying. Who knew why girls cried? One day Kelsey had cried during silent reading just because of the book she had finished! Just because of a made-up thing that happened to a made-up person in a story!

But Izzy had cared when Cody was worried about the pet show. She had brought her friends over to his house to figure out pet costumes. And she had taken such good care of his second-best dog.

As Cody drew nearer to the girls, Kelsey jumped up and practically dragged him over to Izzy.

"I . . . miss . . . Angus!" Izzy choked out the words between sobs. "And I know Angus . . . misses me."

Cody didn't know what to say. "You can come visit him," he offered.

"Last night he slept in my bed!" Izzy wailed.

"He can come for another sleepover," Cody promised. "He can come for lots of sleepovers."

"But then I'll still have to say goodbye. Every single time, I'll have to say goodbye."

There was a long silence.

"Nine pets is a lot," Annika said, as if she were just stating a mathematical fact.

"It's like a story," Kelsey said. "Like a new super-sad ending to the word problem I wrote for Mrs. Molina. Instead of living happily ever after with her princess friends, Princess Izzabella has to be separated from her one true love."

There was another silence.

Cody loved Angus the way he loved Furface, Puffball, Daisy, Doodle, Chicklet, Sir B, and Mr. Piggins. But not the way he loved Rex. He loved Rex more.

He loved Rex the way Izzy loved Angus. And Rex loved Cody the way Angus loved Izzy.

"What about your parents?" he asked Izzy, stalling for time. "Do they like Angus, too?"

"They *love* Angus," Izzy corrected. "When he stayed with me they said it was time for me to get a dog, and I could go to the Humane Society and pick one out. But I said, I don't want *a* dog. I want *this* dog." Her voice was cracking again.

Cody could still be king of pets with eight pets.

A true pet king did whatever would make his pets the happiest.

"I'll talk to my mom and dad," Cody said, "and if they say it's okay—"

Kelsey cut him off. "They will! I know they will!"

Cody knew they would, too.

Izzy leaped up and dashed away. At first Cody was surprised. Why would Izzy run away after he had practically told her that her dream was going to come true? But then, as he saw Izzy tearing around the school track, he got it. She was too happy to stand still.

On she ran. Cody knew she was picturing a little terrier running along beside her.

With a few minutes left in lunch recess, Cody walked over to the fence, hoping to see Stubby. Two other, full-tailed squirrels were nibbling on acorns near the base of the oak tree. They froze in place when Cody appeared, but they didn't flee.

Cody heard someone coming up behind him.

It was Tobit.

"Hey," Cody said cautiously.

"Hey," Tobit replied, his hands thrust into his pockets.

At the sound of their voices, the two squirrels scrabbled up the tree.

To break the awkward silence that followed, Cody picked up a stone. "I call P," he said, and hit the target.

Tobit picked one up, too. "I call *R*." He missed.

Then Cody caught a glimpse of a squirrel with a broken-off tail, atop the section of fence kitty-corner to where the boys were standing.

"It's Stubby," Cody whispered.

Tobit looked in the direction Cody was pointing.

"Do you think he's still mad at me?" Tobit asked in a low voice. "I don't want him to be mad at me."

Cody thought for a moment. "Probably not. I bet he knows you didn't mean it. I bet he knows you won't do it again. Squirrels don't bear grudges. At least, I don't think they do."

Tobit gave a hopeful grin.

"Do you think Sir B would like it if I got him a present?" Tobit asked. "You know, just because?"

"Sure!"

"What kind of food does he like best?" Tobit asked.

Cody didn't have to think about that. "Meal-worms."

"Cool!"

Cody was glad Sir B would get his favorite treat. His pets had won a total of six prizes—six! Angus would get to be loved best in the world by Izzy. Rex would always be loved best in the world by Cody. And Tobit was his friend again.

Pet show day at Franklin School was the best day ever.

Fun Pet Facts

Pet popularity can be judged in different ways. Dogs are the most popular pet in the United States as measured by the number of households with dogs (46.3 percent versus 38.9 percent with cats). But cats are more popular than dogs as measured by the total number of pet cats (95.6 million cats versus 83.3 million dogs). This is because the average cat-owning family has more than one cat. The most popular pet of all, however, measured in sheer numbers, is fish. People in the United States own a total of 142 million pet fish.

The United States has more dogs than any other country in the world. The next four most dog-loving countries are Brazil, China, Russia, and Japan, with the Philippines, India, Argentina, France, and Romania rounding out the top ten.

No one knows for sure when dogs first became domesticated, or tame and able to live side by side with humans. But it was at least ten thousand years ago. Dogs are believed to be the first domesticated animal.

Cats have not been domesticated for as long as dogs, but they were revered in ancient Egypt. Egyptian paintings containing cats date from more than three thousand years ago, and it was a crime in ancient Egypt to harm a cat.

The most popular names for dogs in the United States, according to one survey, are Max, Bella, and Bailey. The most popular names for cats are Bella, Max, and Chloe.

A dog named Laika was the first animal to orbit the earth. She was sent into space by the Soviet Union in 1957 on Sputnik 2. In addition to being astronauts, dogs have also had jobs as sheep-herders, search-and-rescue workers, guides for those with vision, hearing, and mobility chal-lenges, and therapy providers for patients in hospitals and long-term-care facilities.

People who own pets have been shown to live longer and have fewer health problems. Spend-ing time with pets lowers blood pressure, re-lieves stress, and reduces depression.

The TV program *60 Minutes* did a segment in Oc-tober 2014 on "the smartest dog in the world," a border collie named Chaser who is able to iden-tify over one thousand toys by name. Chaser has a vocabulary as big as most human two-year-olds.

Cats have powerful night vision. They can see at light levels six times lower than those human beings need to see by.

A dog's sense of smell has been estimated to be one hundred times keener than a human's.

Many pets have lived in the White House. Abraham Lincoln said that his cat Dixie was "smarter than my whole cabinet." Recent presidential pets include: Barack Obama's Portuguese water dog, Bo; George W. Bush's Scottish terriers, Barney and Miss Beazley; and Chelsea Clinton's cat, Socks.

The Westminster Kennel Club Dog Show, first held in 1877, is America's second-longest continuously held sporting event, behind only the Kentucky Derby.

Labrador retrievers have been the most popular dog breed in the United States for over twenty years. Other popular dog breeds are German shepherds, golden retrievers, beagles, and bulldogs.

Different kinds of pets are found in many countries around the world. In addition to traditional dogs and cats, the Chinese keep crickets. In a crowded city like Beijing, cricket pets don't take up much room. Italy leads Europe in bird ownership; France has more reptile pets than any other European country.

In the United States, there are 6.2 million pet rabbits in 19 million homes and 16 million pet birds in 5.7 million homes.

Americans spend over $50 billion a year on their pets. In fact, they spend over $350 million just on Halloween costumes for their furry companions!

Acknowledgments

Cody needed help from his friends to take all of his pets to the Franklin School pet show. I needed help from my friends to write and publish this book.

My enormously insightful editor, Margaret Ferguson, has an unerring gift of knowing exactly what a story needs to bring it to its best and truest form. Susan Dobinick consistently offers invaluable editorial suggestions as well. After having illustrated four previous Franklin School Friends titles, Rob Shepperson knows my characters even better than I do; I learn something about them from each of his lively, tender drawings.

Thanks also to my ever-encouraging agent, Stephen Fraser; meticulously careful copy editor, Janet Renard; and Elizabeth H. Clark, for the appealing design of the entire series.

Two writer friends are also animal experts. Leslie O'Kane weighed in on dog behavior and offered helpful comments on the entire manuscript. Michelle Begley, rooster lover extraordinaire, is the reason Cody ended up with a rooster as part of his menagerie. Michelle died too soon, in a heartbreaking automobile accident. This book is dedicated to her memory.